U000183879329

D1272541

This book belongs to:

_____

ONCE UPON A gorjuss™ TIME

SANTORO
LONDON

www.santoro-london.com
Gorjuss Collection. ©2006, 2016 Santoro.
Santoro® & Gorjuss™ are trademarks of Santoro.

All rights reserved. No part of this book may be reproduced, transmitted, or stored
in an information retrieval system in any form or by any means, graphic,
electronic, or mechanical, including photocopying, taping, and recording,
without prior written permission from the publisher.

First U.S. edition 2016

Library of Congress Catalog Card Number 2014952795
ISBN 978-0-7636-7742-8

16 17 18 19 20 21 APS 10 9 8 7 6 5 4 3 2 1

Printed in Humen, Dongguan, China

This book was typeset in UglyQua.

Candlewick Entertainment
An imprint of
Candlewick Press
99 Dover Street
Somerville, Massachusetts 02144

visit us at www.candlewick.com

ONCE UPON A gorjuss™ TIME

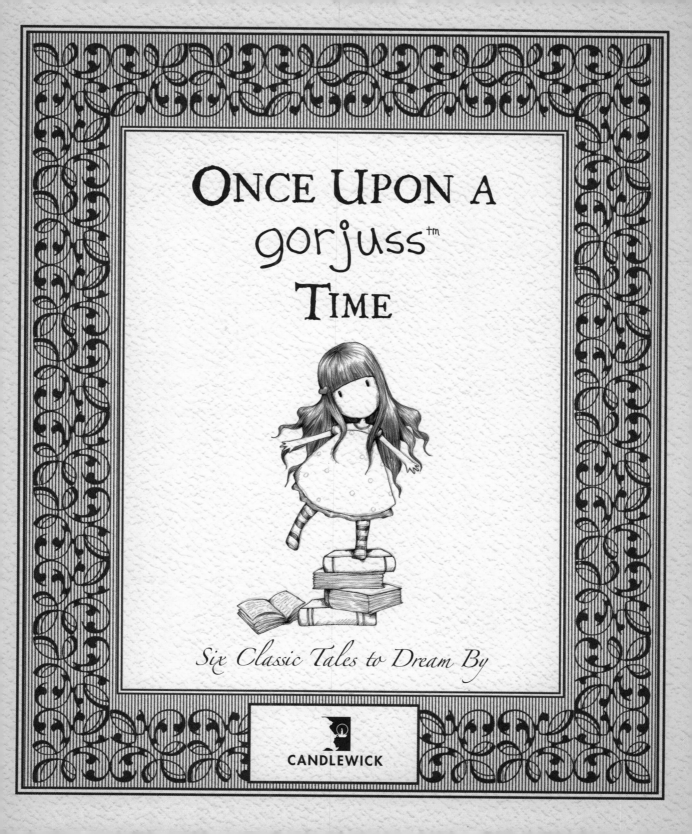

Six Classic Tales to Dream By

CANDLEWICK

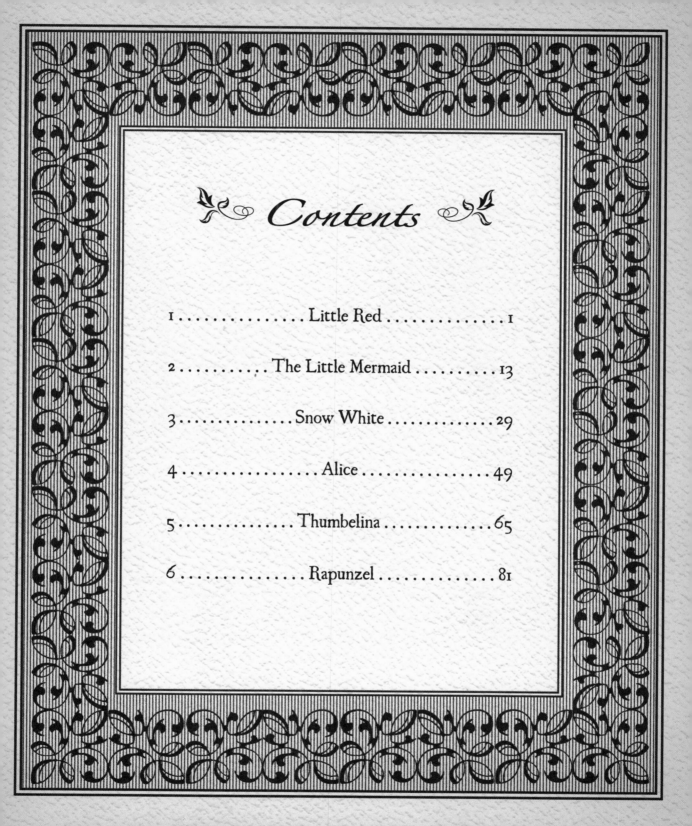

Contents

It's cold and gloomy outside, but in the attic it is cozy, warm, and safe. With piping-hot tea and a plate of scones, the day seems brighter in here somehow. Best of all, there are many books, stacked in tall, higgledy-piggledy piles — so many places to explore.

This old book, a collection of classic tales, is my favorite. I love dressing up and acting out the stories: tiny Thumbelina flying on a bird's back, Alice taking on the Queen of Hearts, dear Little Red venturing out into the forest.... No matter how many times I've read these stories before, I still feel as if I'm reading them for the first time, with me in the main role ... out in the woods, deep in the story.

Ah, and first is the story of Little Red Riding Hood. The forest is a wonderful place, alive with trees and flowers and birds. But there's a sense of danger there, too. Maybe that's what I find so intriguing about this tale....

Little Red

Once upon a time there was a sweet little girl who lived with her father and mother in a pretty cottage surrounded by flowers at the edge of a large forest. At the farthest end of the wood was another cottage. This one was covered in glossy ivy; birds fluttered at its windows, and daisies grew in the front garden. It was here that the girl's grandmother lived.

The little girl was loved by all, for she smiled often and was generous and kind. Grandmother surely loved her more than anyone, and gave her many pretty things. She sewed her granddaughter a beautiful red cloak with a hood that the girl always wore, so people called her Little Red Riding Hood, or Little Red for short.

One morning, Little Red's mother said to her, "Put on your cloak and take this basket to Grandmother. She is ill, so I've made her some cakes, bread, butter, and jam. Go now, and take care in the wood. Stick to the path between the trees."

"I will take great care," promised Little Red.

It was a bright and sunny morning. Little Red Riding Hood was happy to have a chance to walk through the wood. She loved the flowers and birds and woodland

creatures. A friendly fox swished his bushy tail at her ankles as she stopped to pick a bunch of wildflowers for her grandmother. The flowers along the path were trampled, but Little Red spotted some especially beautiful ones between the trees beyond.

Little Red had stooped to pick a pretty flower when she heard a gruff voice behind her: "Good morning, Little Red Riding Hood."

Little Red turned around and saw a great big wolf! He had long sharp teeth, large black eyes, and a very shaggy coat. But

Little Red did not know what a wicked beast the wolf was, so she was not afraid.

"What have you got in that basket, Little Red Riding Hood?" the wolf inquired. When he spoke, it sounded like a deep growl.

"Cakes, bread, butter, and jam," answered the little girl sweetly. She lifted the cloth covering the basket to show him.

"Where are you going with them, my dear?" asked the wolf.

"I am going to visit my grandmother, who is ill," she replied.

"Where does your grandmother live, Little Red Riding Hood?" What a curious wolf he was!

"Along that path, past those wild poppies, then through the gate at the end of the wood. She lives in the pretty little cottage with ivy growing on it and daisies by the door."

This girl is such a tender young creature! the wolf thought to himself. *She will be better to eat than the dry old woman. I must act craftily so as to catch both.*

He walked a short while beside Little Red and then said, "There are even prettier flowers over there beyond that tree.

You must look farther if you would like to pick the best ones." The wolf then said, "Good morning," and set off for Grandmother's cottage.

Little Red continued her search for flowers, and on the wolf's advice went deeper and deeper into the wood. She did  indeed want to take dear Grandmother the loveliest bouquet. After a while, though, she felt tired, so she sat down on a tree stump. Her grandmother's little gray cat appeared through the trees and jumped onto her lap.

Meanwhile, at the farthest edge of the wood, the wolf had reached Grandmother's house. It matched Little Red's description exactly. He banged on the front door.

"Who is it?" called the grandmother.

The wolf tried to speak as sweetly as he could. "It's Little Red Riding Hood, Grandmother."

"Come in, my dear," said the grandmother. "I am too ill to get out of bed."

The wolf stepped inside and found the grandmother in her bedroom. When she saw the wolf, Grandmother became very frightened. She jumped out of bed, dropping her nightcap, and tried to run away. But the wolf was too quick, and he gobbled her up!

The wolf put on the nightcap, crept under the bedclothes, and waited. . . .

In a short while, Little Red Riding Hood arrived at her grandmother's cottage. As the girl crossed the lawn, she saw some striped socks hanging on the washing line. By the front door, she noticed that some  of Grandmother's pretty daisies had been trampled.

Little Red knocked on the door, but there was no answer, so she went inside. "Good morning, Grandmother," she said. "I have brought you cakes, bread, butter, and jam, and here are some flowers I gathered in the wood."

A croaky voice called, "Come here, my dear, for I am too ill to get out of bed."

When Little Red Riding Hood saw her grandmother, she said, "What big ears you have!"

"All the better to hear you with, my dear."

"What big eyes you have, Grandmother!"

"All the better to see you with, my dear."

"But, Grandmother, what a big nose you have!" said the startled girl.

"All the better to smell you with, my dear."

"But, Grandmother, what a big mouth you have!"

"All the better to eat you up with, my dear!" the wolf cried as he sprang at Little Red. He swallowed her down in one large gulp.

His appetite appeased, the wolf lay down again on the bed. Soon he was asleep and snoring loudly, very content.

It happened that a huntsman passed by the house. He heard the wolf's snoring and, thinking it was the poor, sick grandmother, knocked on the door to see if she needed anything. He tried the door and it was unlocked, so he went inside. There he saw the wolf lying in the grandmother's bed.

"What do we have here?" he wondered. He knew immediately that the wolf was a very wicked creature. "You have eaten that dear, sweet grandmother. You have gobbled her up!"

The wolf, who was very tired after his heavy meal, did not stir. The huntsman took up a pair of scissors and carefully cut open the stomach of the sleeping wolf so that the grandmother might be saved. He made two snips, and out popped Little Red.

"Oh, how frightened I have been," she said. "That wolf swallowed me in one big bite. How dark it was inside his belly!"

The huntsman made two snips more, and out came Little Red's dear grandmother. She was shaken, but Little Red comforted her with some of the sweet treats she had brought along.

The grandmother recovered her spirits and then hugged Little Red tight, for her dearest granddaughter was safe.

When Little Red was sure that Grandmother was well, she went outside and collected six large mushrooms. She carried them to the huntsman, who was standing guard by the sleeping wolf.

"Put these inside his belly," Little Red said to the huntsman. "And sew him up. Then he will not know that we are free."

The huntsman did as Little Red bid.

No sooner had he sewn the last stitch than the wolf awoke. Little Red and her grandmother hid so the wolf would not see them. The huntsman waved his ax, and the wolf growled before leaping out of the window and disappearing into the forest.

Little Red did not know that the mushrooms she had picked were poisonous. Soon the wicked wolf sickened and died.

In the cottage, the huntsman, Little Red, and her grandmother all sat down to celebrate and enjoy the cakes and bread that Little Red's mother had sent. As they ate, Little Red thought to herself, *I will never leave the path to run into the wood when my mother has forbidden me to do so.*

Little Red visited her grandmother many times from that day on, but she always stuck to the path.

THE END

Oh, what a wonderful story, and so deliciously frightening.
In this world of varied dangers, we are all Little Reds,
and we are wise to beware. . . .

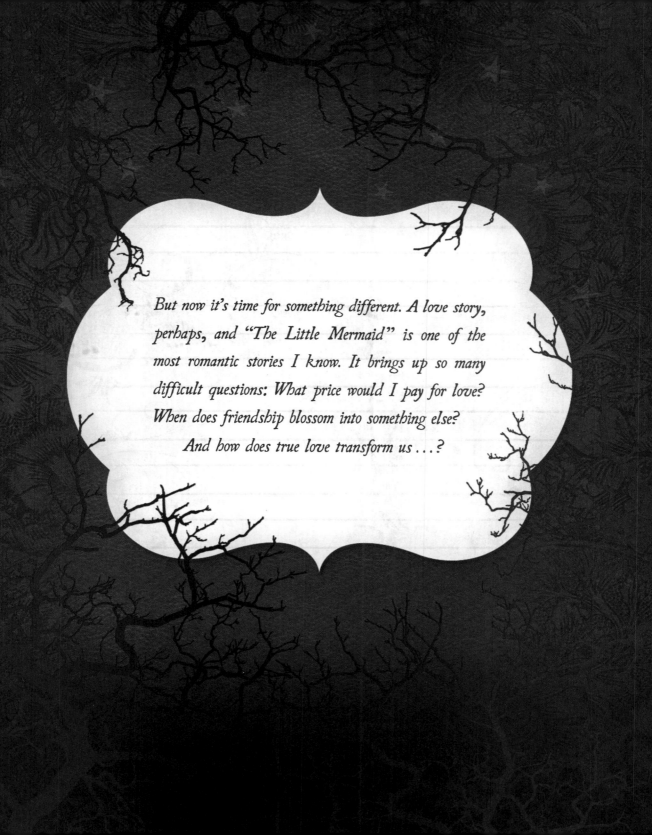

But now it's time for something different. A love story, perhaps, and "The Little Mermaid" is one of the most romantic stories I know. It brings up so many difficult questions: What price would I pay for love? When does friendship blossom into something else?

And how does true love transform us . . . ?

The Little Mermaid

Perhaps you've heard seafaring tales from sailors, those who say they've seen mermaids frolicking in the waves, or heard voices singing just as a storm rolls in across the water. Are these tricks of the exhausted mind?

No! Such tales are likely true, for far from shore and deep below the ocean's surface there is indeed a kingdom of merfolk. The Sea King lives there in a palace of amber, coral, and pearls, and his daughters are more beautiful than any creature that walks upon land, though their bodies end in fish tails rather than legs.

Years ago, when the Sea King's four daughters were very young, they were cared for by their grandmother, for their own mother had died. The girls played in the palace halls, darting among flowers that grew out of the walls and colorful fish that

roamed freely inside. Their grandmother allotted each of them a plot of ground just outside the castle walls in which to plant a garden. The eldest daughters shaped their flower beds as a whale, a starfish, and an oyster shell, but the youngest planted hers round like the sun, with flaming yellow, orange, and red sea blossoms. In the middle she placed a marble statue of a handsome boy, which had fallen down to the watery depths from a shipwreck.

The little mermaid was desperately curious about the world above, and she begged her grandmother to share all she knew of towns, people, and animals. As she grew older, the little mermaid would swim closer and closer to the surface to try to catch glimpses of the boats drifting above. She would collect whatever human objects sank to the ocean floor: a broken sextant, a cracked fiddle, a wide hat.

One fateful evening, the little mermaid rose higher than ever before and broke through the surface of the sea.

She marveled at the sky, and heard joyful music floating down from a passing ship. Intrigued, she swam up to the portholes to peer inside. A party was in full swing, with sailors dancing, clapping, and cheering. In their midst was a beautiful prince. The little mermaid was mesmerized by the sight of him. She had never before seen anyone so handsome.

As she clung to the side of the ship and watched the festivities, the sky darkened and the waves began to rise higher and higher. A storm had come!

The party ended abruptly as the sailors ran to their posts, pulling on ropes and lashing barrels to the deck. But the wind blew too fiercely, and the ship rocked violently upon the turbulent waters. Lightning flashed, the sails lit up with flames, and the ship tumbled upon a rock. It burst apart into a thousand ragged pieces.

The little mermaid swam quickly under the water and found the unconscious prince drowning. Desperate to save him, the mermaid pulled him up to the surface and then swam with him, for mile after mile, toward shore.

She left him on a beach but kept watching from the sea until a young girl passed by. The girl rushed over to the prince's body and managed to revive him. She screamed for help, and soon afterward a group of men arrived and carried the weakened prince away.

The mermaid reluctantly slipped back into the waves and returned home.

Back in the undersea kingdom, the little mermaid was distracted. She pined for the handsome prince, and no amount of spectacle and gaiety at the palace would turn her thoughts away from him. Finally, one night, while her sisters were busy dancing and singing at a court ball, the mermaid slipped away to seek an old merwoman who years before had been cast out of the Sea King's realm. She found the notorious woman in a dark hollow. Scores of sea snakes slithered about her.

"Please," begged the little mermaid, "you must help me find a way to become human. How else can I win the prince's heart?"

The merwoman pulled a book of ancient recipes off the shelf. "I can brew a draft for you, although it would be foolish of you to drink it. It rids you of your fish tail, and instead gives you legs. You would be very graceful, but you would feel as though you were treading on sharp knives with every step."

"I'll drink it," said the mermaid, because she loved the prince very much, although in truth she was frightened.

"As you like," replied the old merwoman. "But remember, if the prince gives his heart to another, you will dissolve and become no more than foam on the crest of waves."

Of course, the merwoman would not give the young maiden the draft for free; she demanded the little mermaid's voice as payment.

The mermaid returned to the shore where she had left the prince. With great trepidation, she drank the draft. At first nothing happened, but then suddenly she tensed and opened her mouth in a silent scream — she felt pure agony, as though a hot sword were cutting her in half! She fell into a dead faint.

When she awoke, the little mermaid looked down to find she was now human, with two sturdy legs.

A moment later, who should come by but the prince himself! He had returned to the scene of his own rescue, compelled by the vague memory of a pretty young girl. He did not find the girl he sought, but instead came upon the little mermaid, who only appeared to be a mute girl in need of his help.

He picked up the little mermaid and carried her back to his castle, where she was dressed in costly robes of silk. The prince was delighted by this mysterious, silent beauty, and he brought her along to the palace entertainment that evening.

The little mermaid listened with no small amount of sorrow to the choir. Their harmonies soared, and she longed to sing — to speak! — but could only look on. Then, when the dancing began, the mermaid floated onto the floor, charming everyone with her beauty and grace. No one realized that the mermaid suffered great pain with each step.

After a short while, the mermaid could bear it no longer. She slipped out of the hall and into the empty courtyard, where she took off her shoes and bathed her poor feet in the cooling waters of a fountain.

The mermaid suffered great pain with each step.

The little mermaid remained in the palace, and as time passed the prince grew very fond of her. They traveled his kingdom together and became very close. But the prince was still haunted by his memory of the girl from the beach, and he could not give away his heart.

The mermaid's own heart cracked at this realization, but she held out hope that he would grow to love her nonetheless.

The king and queen began to worry about the prince's future. The strange mute girl who kept him company would not do as a proper princess. So, in the hope of a better match, they arranged for the prince to call on a neighboring kingdom, where the crown princess was rumored to be very beautiful.

The prince and his entourage boarded a ship, and of course the little mermaid went with them. As they sailed over the waters, the prince told his mute companion of the strange fish that swam far beneath the surface. The mermaid smiled, for she knew better than anyone what lurked beneath the sea. It pained her, too, for she longed to see her family again, most especially her sisters.

When the prince went belowdecks, the little mermaid saw some movement near the horizon. She could just make out her sisters among the choppy waters, waving to her. She felt cheered to see them, if only for a moment.

When the ship docked in the harbor of the adjoining kingdom, the prince was greeted by a flourish of trumpets. A festival had been prepared for him.

When the crown princess arrived, the little mermaid had to admit that the girl was indeed very beautiful, with large dark eyes and delicate skin.

The prince was beside himself. "It was you," he cried, "who saved my life on the beach!" He embraced the princess.

It was true: she was the same girl who had come upon his half-drowned body on the beach, for she had been sent abroad for her education. The fissure in the little mermaid's heart split wide open, because she knew that her prince loved the princess.

She felt stabbing pains with each graceful twirl.

The prince and princess arranged to be married, and the ceremony was planned for the very next week. It took place on the prince's ship amid cannons firing and great jubilation. The couple exchanged their solemn vows.

That night, the mermaid danced as she had never danced before, and the crowd cheered her on. She felt stabbing pains with each graceful twirl, but she cared not, for her heart held far greater suffering.

As the bridal pair slept in a costly tent of purple and gold on deck, the mermaid looked out toward the deep blue horizon, dreading sunrise, when she was destined to perish and become foam upon the sea.

Suddenly she heard her name — her mermaid name — from below. She looked down into the dark waters, and there were her sisters, all with their hair cut off.

"We have struck a bargain with the old merwoman," they cried. "We have traded our hair for this knife. If you plunge it into the prince's heart, then you shall be saved. You will have your fish tail back, and you can return home with us.

Our father and grandmother miss you dearly. Oh, do hurry, for you must kill him before the sun rises."

The mermaids disappeared beneath the water.

The little mermaid, the sharp knife held in her trembling hand, drew back the heavy purple curtain of the bridal tent. There she saw the fair bride, her head resting upon the prince's chest. The prince was the mermaid's own true love, the man for whom she longed, and for whom she had suffered.

It was nearly dawn. The mermaid knew there was only one thing for her to do: she flung the knife into the sea, and then jumped in after it. Her body dissolved into foam.

But the little mermaid did not die. Instead she rose, quiet as a bubble, from the sea. She drifted over the ship and ascended ever higher into the sky. The dawn flamed pink, and the night retreated. But moments before the last star faded into blue, one could see a quick pinprick of light. A new star had flashed into being.

THE END

Sorrow and pain are truly horrible, but they reveal depths inside us that
we might not have seen before. I suppose mighty kings and fearsome
knights can be powerful in their way, but the little mermaid
has shown a strength that is boundless.

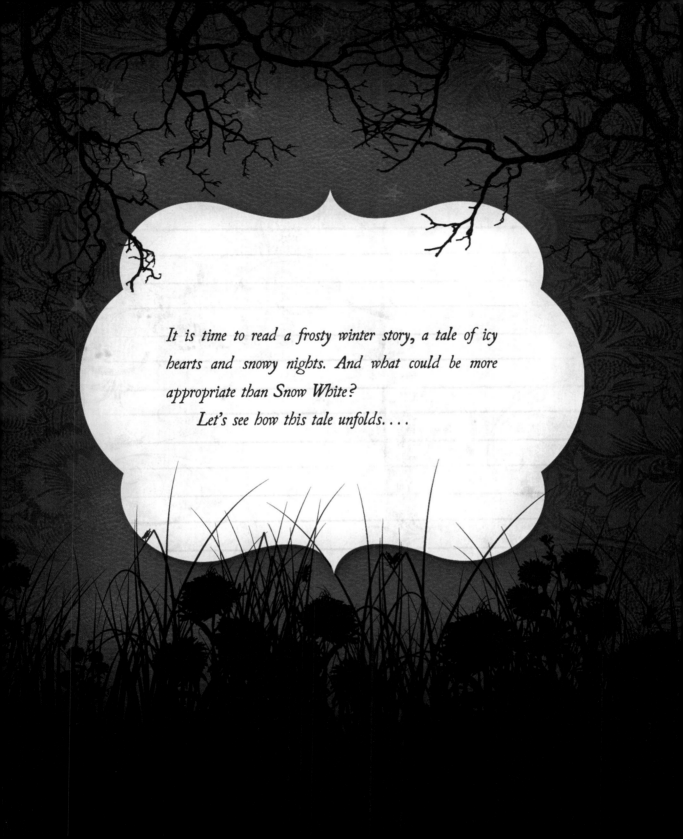

It is time to read a frosty winter story, a tale of icy hearts and snowy nights. And what could be more appropriate than Snow White?

Let's see how this tale unfolds. . . .

Snow White

It was the middle of winter, and a blanket of snow lay heavy against the stately walls of a castle far away in the wood. The palace had high turrets built of strongest granite, and its ebony-framed windows reflected the falling snow. The queen sat at one of those windows, embroidering a tiny sleeping cap for her unborn child. She looked out upon the swirling white beyond, mesmerized, and accidentally pricked her finger on the needle. Three drops of blood fell into her lap. The queen said, "Would that my daughter be as white as that snow, as red as that blood, and as black as that window frame."

Soon after, the queen gave birth to a beautiful baby girl with hair as black as ebony, skin as white as snow, and cheeks as rosy as blood. The queen named her Snow White.

Snow White loved her mother dearly, and they were always together in the palace gardens, laughing among the flowers. But in Snow White's eighth winter, her mother died.

Snow White was beset with grief.

The king married again shortly after. The new queen was very beautiful but very proud, and she could not bear the thought that anyone's beauty should surpass her own.

She would gaze into her looking glass and ask:

"Oh, mirror, tell me, tell me,
  Of all the ladies in this fair land,
Who is the fairest?
Tell me. Tell me, who?"

And the mirror always answered:

"You, dear Queen,
  You are the fairest in all the land."

The new queen was happy then because she was truly the most beautiful.

But Snow White's pretty appearance slowly matured into something more, day after day. The girl's kindness grew, too, and she loved to play in the royal gardens, remembering her mother's laugh. The summer birds and palace cats kept her company.

Snow White turned eighteen during the longest winter the kingdom had ever seen. The white snow made her skin appear even paler, her hair darker, and her cheeks rosier.

The queen continued to consult her mirror on who was the fairest in the land. One day, the glass answered:

"You, dear Queen, may be fair and beautiful,
But Snow White is lovelier even than you."

When the queen heard this, she flew into a terrible rage. She ordered one of the king's guards to take Snow White deep into the dark forest and kill her. "She must not live another day!" the queen cried.

It carried her farther into the darkness.

The guard led the girl far into the wood, but when he looked at her, his heart melted. "I cannot hurt you, sweet one," he said. "Run, hide in the forest, and never return to the palace."

The man felt a heavy weight in his heart as he watched the girl flee. A wild beast would most likely find her and tear her to pieces, but he consoled himself that she had not died by his hand.

Snow White wandered the wood in great fear. Soon night fell, and she became very tired, but there was nowhere to rest. Finally, she collapsed under a tree, shivering — although whether from cold or terror, she could not say. She closed her eyes, defeated.

Just then a fawn emerged from the dark wood. It knelt and nuzzled against Snow White, encouraging her to mount. She crawled gratefully upon the fawn's back, and it stood. It carried her farther into the darkness, until the passing branches lulled the girl to sleep, still clinging to the kind animal's neck.

The next morning, Snow White awoke to the sight of seven dwarves standing over her. They were delighted to have found her. "My, what a pretty girl she is!" one said. Snow White was frightened, but the dwarves assured her that she had nothing to fear from them.

Snow White told them that the evil queen had ordered her killed. The dwarves pitied her and invited her to their little house just over the hill. If she would keep all their things neatly ordered, cook and wash for them, mend their clothes, and knit them little jackets in the winter, then she could stay with them for as long as she liked.

Snow White agreed, and she followed the dwarves over the hill. Their little blue house had seven windows and a bright white door. Inside, everything was orderly. The table was spread with a white cloth, upon which sat seven little glasses and seven little plates with seven loaves and seven sets of cutlery. In the bedroom upstairs there was a line of seven little beds.

The dwarves lighted seven lamps and sat down to eat. Each dwarf gave Snow White a small piece of his own loaf so that she would not go hungry.

The dwarves worked all day long in the mountains, digging for gold and silver. Snow White remained at home, and they warned her not to open the door to anyone. "The queen will soon find out where you are. You must stay safe inside."

In the palace on the other side of the kingdom, the queen consulted her looking glass. "Am I the fairest in all the land?" she asked.

And the glass answered:

"You, dear Queen, are the loveliest in the land.
But over the hills, in the deepest part of the wood,
Where the seven dwarves their dwelling have made,
There Snow White is hiding; and she
Is more beautiful, dear Queen, even than you."

Then the queen was very angry because she knew the guardsman had betrayed her; her glass always spoke the truth. She could not trust any of the palace servants, so she disguised herself as an old peasant woman and trekked deep into the forest herself to find the dwarves' home.

When she arrived at the little blue house, she knocked at the door and cried, "Fine wares to sell!"

Snow White looked out of the window and said, "Good day, good woman. What have you to sell?"

"Good wares, fine wares," replied the old woman. "Ribbons and buttons and laces of all colors."

Snow White thought to herself, *I will let the old lady in, for she seems to be a very good sort, and I should so like a new ribbon for my dress.*

When Snow White opened the door, the old peasant woman said, "My, what a beautiful child you are! I have just the thing for you." And from her basket she pulled out a pretty, striped ribbon. "Let me tie this for you."

Snow White stood before the old woman, who set to work nimbly, pulling the ribbon tight around Snow White's delicate waist — so tight that she lost her breath and fell down in a deathly faint.

The queen laughed. "There's the end of all your beauty," she said, and began her journey back to the palace. The animals of the forest gathered around Snow White, but none could wake her up.

In the evening when the seven dwarves returned from work, they were grieved to see their kind and beautiful Snow White stretched out upon the ground as if quite dead.

"The queen has been here," said one, as the others lifted Snow White and carried her into the house. Once inside, they noticed the new ribbon. As soon as they cut it, Snow White began to breathe. Soon she was herself again.

The dwarves warned her again that she must not let anyone into the house. "The queen knows where you are. You must stay safe inside."

Snow White cried for her foolishness and promised to heed their words.

When the queen arrived back at the palace, she went to her looking glass and spoke to it. To her surprise, it replied as before that the queen was indeed lovely but that far away in the forest lived Snow White, who was even more beautiful.

The queen's blood ran cold to hear that Snow White still lived. The next day, she dressed again in disguise, but a very different one from the one she wore before. She went to her secret cupboard and removed a poison comb.

When the disguised queen reached the dwarves' cottage for a second time, she knocked at the door, crying, "Beautiful jewelry and hair combs for sale!"

Snow White came to the door, but remembering the dwarves' wise words, said, "I dare not let anyone in."

And the black-hearted queen replied, "Only look at my beautiful combs, my dear. This one is shaped like a dragonfly. How pretty it will look on you." The disguised queen held up the poison comb.

It is indeed very pretty, thought Snow White, and she took the comb and put it in her hair. But the moment it touched her head she fell down senseless, for the poison was very powerful.

"There you may lie," cackled the queen, and went on her way.

By a turn of good fortune, the dwarves returned home early that evening. They knew immediately that the queen had been there, and they quickly spotted the comb. As soon as they had pulled it from Snow White's hair she began to recover.

They warned her again, "The queen knows you are here. You must stay inside to be safe."

Meanwhile, the queen went home to her glass. She screamed in rage as she received the same answer as before.

"Snow White shall die," she cried, "if it costs me my life!"

So she went for a third time to her secret chamber and there prepared a poisoned apple. Its outside was rosy and tempting, but anyone who tasted the fruit was sure to die.

She dressed herself up again, this time as a farmer's wife, and went once more to the little cottage in the wood.

She knocked at the door, but Snow White did not come. Instead Snow White opened a window, for she remembered well the dwarves' wise words. "I dare not let anyone in."

The queen begged, but Snow White refused.

"You silly girl!" the queen cried. "What are you afraid of? Do you think it is poisoned? Come! Do you not want to eat such a pretty fruit? You eat one part, and I will eat the other."

Now, the apple was so prepared that one side was good, and the other side was poisoned.

Snow White was tempted to taste the apple, for it looked exceedingly juicy. She waited until the farmer's wife had taken a bite and then she tasted it herself. She fell down dead.

"This time nothing will save you," gloated the queen, and she went home to the palace to consult her looking glass.

"You, dear Queen, are the fairest in all the land," it said.

The queen sang and danced with gladness, for Snow White was dead and the queen was once again the most beautiful in all the kingdom.

When evening came and the dwarves returned home, they found Snow White lying on the ground. This time there was no ribbon to cut and no comb to remove. Snow White lay cold and still as stone.

Snow White was tempted to taste the apple.

41

The dwarves cried as they laid her to rest in a field of flowers, with a silver plaque that named her as the king's daughter. The creatures of the wood all came to mourn poor dead Snow White — an owl, a fox cub, a songbird.

Snow White lay among the woodland flowers for many months and still looked only as if she were sleeping. Her skin stayed as white as snow, her hair as black as ebony, and her cheeks as red as blood.

One day, a prince was riding through the forest when he saw Snow White. He read what was written on the plaque, and his heart was filled with pity for the beautiful dead girl and for her father. He begged the dwarves to let him carry her back to the palace, to which they sorrowfully agreed.

As he lifted Snow White to place her upon his horse, a piece of apple fell from her sweet mouth.

Snow White awoke and cried, "Where am I?"

The dwarves and the prince were greatly astonished, and they explained all that had happened.

"Come with me," said the prince to the girl. "I will take you safely home to the palace."

Snow White, who longed to see her father again, agreed, and they rode through the forest together. The king was glad to see his beautiful daughter again, for he had been crippled with mourning since the day she disappeared. When he learned about his wife's betrayal and her attempts to kill Snow White, he grew very angry. His advisers told him that the queen must be put to death for her treachery, but the king was a kindhearted man and did not want to see her killed. Instead, he ordered that she be taken from the palace to live in a tiny cottage on the edge of the wood, where she would be guarded day and night. She took her mirror with her, but she never consulted it again.

A year passed, during which Snow White spent much time with her father. They talked and talked, and it broke her father's heart to hear of the great sorrow that Snow White had suffered. She assured him that all was forgotten now that she was safe. The prince was a regular visitor at the palace, and slowly he and Snow White fell in love. They were married during Snow White's twentieth year. When the king sadly sickened and died three winters later, they ascended to the throne. They reigned happily over the kingdom together for the rest of their lives.

THE END

What a terrific tale, and I do love happy endings.
This story has such truth in it, for a beautiful face might be
a wonderful gift, but real beauty comes from within.

These stories really bring to light the power of words, and the deep feelings they can provoke.

But words can bring great fun too. I dearly love to laugh, and so next I shall turn to this story, which has turned wild flights of imagination into a timeless classic, an adventure full of surprises.

Alice

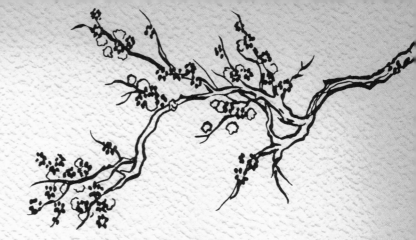

One lazy summer's day, Alice sat with her sister on a riverbank. She was bored. In her hands was a daisy. She spun the stem, first clockwise, then back. For a moment she considered picking more flowers and weaving a crown for herself . . . but she couldn't be bothered. It was too hot. There was barely a breeze rocking the leafy branches above.

Suddenly a movement caught her eye: a rabbit, running along the bank. At first Alice wasn't particularly surprised — there were many rabbits about — and even when he exclaimed, "Oh, dear! Oh, dear! I shall be too late!" she didn't find it strange. (Although, when she thought about it later, she realized it *was* strange.)

But then the rabbit checked his pocket watch, and Alice was on her feet in a flash, running after the odd fellow. After all, she had never before seen a rabbit carrying a pocket watch! The rabbit leaped into a large rabbit hole under a hedge, his pocket watch trailing behind on a long, thin chain, and in another moment Alice tumbled down after him. So intent was she on the chase that she didn't even consider how she would ever climb out again.

Alice fell down the hole, farther and farther, the earth walls flying up above her. Pebbles and roots zipped past her in the growing darkness, but soon the tunnel walls became smooth, almost as if they were finished in plaster. Then, curiously, she fell past what appeared to be wooden paneling, and — *oh!* There was a book, sitting up on a shelf. And another.

Soon she was falling past a whole series of stacked bookshelves, upon which the books themselves rose up in messy piles. She plucked a book as she fell past, paged through the illustrations, and then placed it back on another shelf, many feet below the first. There were other things, too — a collection of brass buttons, a pack of cards — and she began to wonder, *Will I ever stop falling?*

Alice's question was soon answered, for suddenly — *thump! Thump!* — down she came upon a pile of soft, green leaves. It was quite lucky she fell there, for she was not a bit hurt. No sooner had she hit the bottom than she sprang up and looked about her. She caught a glimpse of the rabbit, far off, turning down a narrow passage, and she broke into a run after him.

"Oh, my ears and whiskers, how late it's getting!" she heard, just as the rabbit disappeared.

Alice found herself in a long hall with a row of doors on either side. She tried all the doors, but they were all locked.

How will I ever get out? she wondered.

Just then, she spotted a small three-legged table made of glass. Something twinkled upon it; Alice looked closer and saw that it was a tiny brass key, no bigger than her thumbnail. *How strange,* she thought. *What could it be for?*

She looked around and noticed that there was a tiny door located along the bottom edge of the wall. It was only about fifteen inches high. *That must be it!*

Excited, Alice took the tiny key and tried the lock in the small door. It opened, and she knelt down to look through the doorway. Beyond was the loveliest garden she had ever seen. Alice longed to walk among the bright flowers and cool trees, but she could not even fit her head through the door.

Disappointed, she shut the door again, stood back up, and walked over to the small table. To her surprise, she found a teacup with the words "DRINK ME" written upon a tag. She was getting quite thirsty, so she dropped the key in her pocket and ventured to taste the tea.

"What a curious feeling!" she cried as the room around her suddenly grew enormous. Or perhaps not — she was shrinking! Down, down, down she went, until she was just the right size for the door. She drew the key from her pocket, unlocked the door, and ventured into the garden beyond.

Alice wandered among the flowers, reveling in their cheerful colors. She picked some red tulips and gathered them together in a basket that had been left lying in the sun. She closed her eyes, taking in the sweet scents wafting through the air.

The room around her suddenly grew enormous.

When she opened her eyes again, she was surprised to see a cat sitting in a tree just above her. It was a rather large cat, and, strangely, it was grinning from ear to ear.

"I wonder why it grins?" she said to herself aloud.

"I'm a Cheshire cat," replied the animal, much to Alice's surprise. "That's why."

Alice didn't quite know what to say. She paused uncomfortably, then ventured, "Could you please tell me which way I ought to go from here? I don't much care where, so long as I get somewhere."

"Oh, you're sure to do that," the cat replied, "if you only walk long enough. In that direction lives the March Hare. He's quite mad."

"But I don't want to go among mad people," said Alice.

"Oh, you can't help that, we're all mad here in Wonderland. I'm mad, you're mad."

"How do you know I'm mad?"

"You must be," said the cat, "or you wouldn't have come here." The cat's tail began to vanish, then its body, then its head, and ending with its toothy grin, which remained hanging in the air some time after the rest had gone.

"Curiouser and curiouser," muttered Alice, as she picked up her basket of flowers and headed in the direction of the March Hare; after all, she didn't know where else to go.

Alice soon came upon a table laid out for tea. It was a rather large table, but at one end crowded the March Hare, the Hatter, and the Dormouse.

"No room! No room!" they cried out when they saw Alice coming.

"There's plenty of room!" said Alice, indignant, and she sat down in one of the large armchairs.

The Hatter turned to her. "Why is a raven like a writing desk?"

Alice pondered the question. Then she noticed the Hatter's watch. "What a funny watch," she remarked. "It tells the day of the month, but not the hour!"

"Why should it?" he replied. "Time and I have quarreled, so it's always six o'clock now."

"Teatime," added the March Hare.

"Why did you quarrel?" inquired Alice.

"At the great concert given by the Queen of Hearts, I sang:

'Twinkle, twinkle, little bat!
How I wonder what you're at!
Up above the world you fly,
Like a tea-tray in the sky.'"

The Dormouse's head slumped against the table. He was fast asleep.

The Hatter continued, "I had hardly finished the first verse when the queen jumped up and cried, 'He's murdering time! Off with his head!'"

"Oh, dear!" exclaimed Alice.

"I want a clean cup," stated the Hatter abruptly. He moved over to the next chair, as the Dormouse woke up and moved to his right. The March Hare took the Dormouse's place, and Alice rather unwillingly moved into the March Hare's seat.

"Have you guessed the riddle yet?" asked the Hatter.

"No, I give up," Alice replied. "What's the answer?"

"I have no idea," he said.

"Nor I," said the March Hare.

Alice sighed wearily. "A riddle with no answer? I don't think—"

"Then you shouldn't talk," snapped the Hatter.

Madness was one thing, but rudeness was more than Alice could bear. She got up from the table and stalked back toward the garden.

An odd sight greeted Alice by the garden's entrance. A large rose tree stood nearby, and three playing cards were applying red paint to the tree's blooms, which were white.

"Pardon me, but why are you painting those roses?" asked Alice. "I think they look just as lovely white."

The cards looked uneasily at one another, and then the Two of Spades replied, "The fact is, miss, this here ought to have been a red rose tree, but we put a white one in by mistake. If the queen was to find out, we should all have our heads cut off, you know."

The whole pack rose up in the air.

Just then, a peal of trumpets sounded, and a call was heard: "The queen! The queen!" The three gardeners instantly threw themselves flat upon the ground.

A procession arrived, led by the Queen of Hearts. The queen spotted Alice, who remained standing, and said severely, "Who is this? What is your name, child?"

"My name is Alice, so please Your Majesty," she said.

"But who are these?" The queen pointed to the three cards lying on the ground; for, you see, as they were lying on their faces, the pattern on their backs was the same as the rest.

"How should I know?" responded Alice, surprised at her own courage. "It's no business of mine."

Gasps were heard throughout the procession. The queen flushed with fury, glaring at Alice. Then she screamed, "Off with her head! Off with her head!"

"Nonsense!" said Alice, very loudly and decidedly. Nobody moved. Encouraged, Alice continued, "Who cares for you? You're nothing but a pack of cards!"

At this the whole pack rose up in the air and came flying down upon Alice. She tried to beat them off, and suddenly found herself lying on the riverbank with her head in the lap of her sister, who was gently brushing away some dead leaves that had fluttered down from the trees.

"Wake up, Alice dear," said her sister. "What a long sleep you've had."

"Oh," replied Alice, looking about in wonder. "I've had such a curious dream."

THE END

Wonderland was just a dream.

I suppose that should come as no surprise:

dreams are the seeds for all things wonderful!

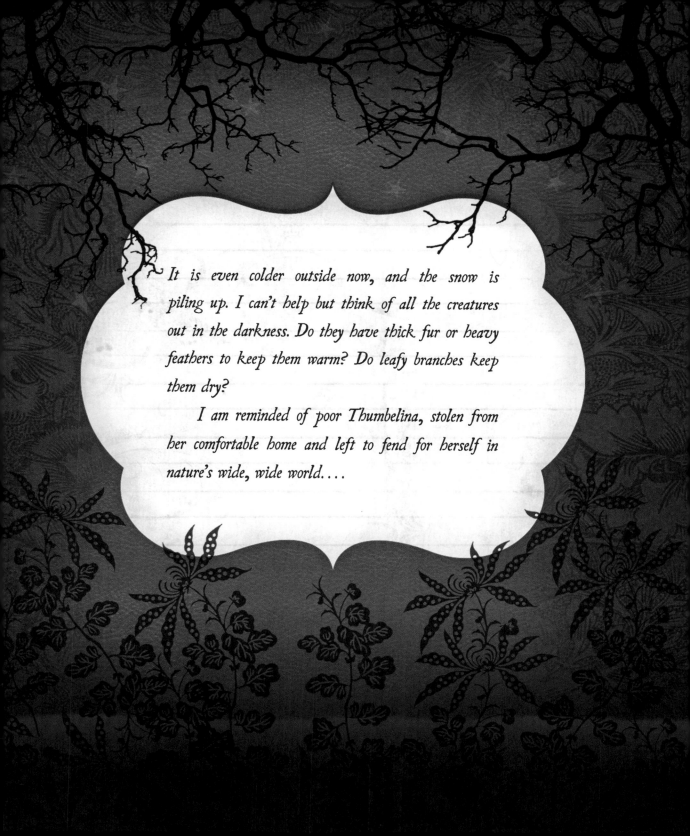

It is even colder outside now, and the snow is piling up. I can't help but think of all the creatures out in the darkness. Do they have thick fur or heavy feathers to keep them warm? Do leafy branches keep them dry?

I am reminded of poor Thumbelina, stolen from her comfortable home and left to fend for herself in nature's wide, wide world....

Thumbelina

ong ago there was a peasant woman who lived alone near a sleepy pond, with only birds and lilies and trees for company. All she wanted was a child to love and care for, someone to brighten her modest home. She sought out a wise old woman deep in the dark wood and begged for help. The old woman took pity on her and handed her a barleycorn. "This is no ordinary grain," she said. "Plant it, and see what happens."

The lonely peasant returned home to the pond. She planted the barleycorn in a pot, which she lovingly wrapped with a bow. Soon a large, exquisite flower grew. The bloom looked like a rosebud or a tulip, with its bright pink velvet petals. They were pressed tightly together, as if guarding a precious secret.

The woman was overcome by its loveliness and cried out in delight. "How beautiful," she said, and she gently kissed the petals.

As she did so, the flower opened.

Inside sat a tiny girl, only about half as long as a thumb. The woman called her Little Thumb, or Thumbelina.

The girl was beautiful and delicate, and she sang so sweetly that all who heard her song fell in love with her.

The peasant woman spent what few coins she had on scraps of fine silks, buttons, and lace, from which she sewed pretty clothes for Thumbelina. She made a warm bath for her new daughter in one teacup and filled another with rose petals to serve as a bed.

One night, while Thumbelina lay sleeping, a large, ugly toad crept through a broken window and slopped up to her scented teacup bed. Earlier that day, the toad had heard Thumbelina's sweet song, and he wanted to marry her.

He took up Thumbelina and carried her out the window and into the garden. There he waddled to the edge of the pond and placed Thumbelina down upon a lily pad. Then he hopped into the water, among the fish, and dragged the leaf away from the mucky shore.

The tiny girl woke very early the next morning. When she looked about her and saw that she was far from home, she began to cry.

The hideous toad spread his lips in a smile and croaked, "You will marry me tonight." Then he swam away to make his wedding preparations, leaving Thumbelina all alone on the lily pad. It was too far for her to swim to the bank.

Thumbelina wept for a long time. A pink butterfly heard the girl's plaintive sobs, and he alighted on the lily pad to hear her unhappy tale. The fish swimming below felt pity, too, and they began to nibble at the green stem that held the girl's pad rooted in place.

When the lily leaf was no longer tethered, Thumbelina took the striped ribbon from her waist. She gave one end of

it to the butterfly and tied the other to the leaf. The butterfly took to the air, and Thumbelina's leaf was pulled downstream and into the wild unknown.

As the butterfly towed Thumbelina to safety, she sang him songs to encourage him. A large ladybug heard her song and immediately fell in love with her. He swooped down to catch Thumbelina by her tiny waist and flew with her to a nearby tree.

The other ladybugs that lived in the tree stared at Thumbelina and exclaimed, "But she only has two legs! It's unfortunate that she looks so much like a human being. They're ever so ugly."

The large ladybug who had stolen poor Thumbelina was embarrassed that he had ever cared for her. He flew her down from the tree, placed her on a daisy, and took off.

Thumbelina sobbed at the thought that she was ugly, although in truth she was the loveliest girl ever seen.

Poor little Thumbelina was left to fend for herself in the forest. She wove a bed from blades of grass and slept under a broad leaf to keep dry. She drank nectar from wildflowers for strength and quenched her thirst with morning dew.

Summer passed into autumn, and a chill crept over the land. Thumbelina watched the birds fly for warmer lands and the flowers wither around her. Even the leaf that protected her from rain shriveled up, and she was left exposed to the dreadful cold.

Thumbelina shivered in the freezing wind as it whipped through her clothes, once so fine but now worn threadbare. She climbed over icy branches and mounds of feathery snow, slipping and stumbling forward, not knowing where to find shelter.

She came at last to a burrow. She fell knocking upon the door, teeth chattering. She could feel her life slipping away. At long last, the door opened and a hedgehog stood before her.

"You poor desperate creature!" the hedgehog exclaimed. "Please come inside and warm yourself at my hearth.

Winter is not a favorable time for wanderers; you must stay here with me until spring."

The hedgehog kept a comfortable home, and Thumbelina was glad of her company. She told the hedgehog stories in the evenings, and sang lilting lullabies at night. It was a happy time.

"We shall have a visitor today," announced the hedgehog one fine morning. "My neighbor, the mole, comes to visit often. He is very rich and learned, with a beautiful black velvet coat. But he is blind. You must tell him your pretty stories of the world."

The mole arrived shortly afterward, coming through a tunnel he had dug from his own home.

Thumbelina was obliged to tell him stories and sing him a cheerful song. The mole had no interest in Thumbelina's tales of sunshine or colorful flowers, but he fell in love with the girl for her sparkling voice.

One night when Thumbelina couldn't sleep, she took an underground walk down the tunnel that the mole had built. She came across a fine bluebird lying perfectly still, evidently dead from the cold, outside the mole's front door.

Filled with pity, Thumbelina wove a delicate carpet of hay and laid it over the bird as a shroud. She kissed the bird's closed eyelids and rested her head upon his breast, humming a song of summer.

Thump! Thump! Thump!

It was the bird's heart.

He was not really dead, only numb with cold, and her blanket had warmed him. Glad that the bird was alive, Thumbelina dashed back to the hedgehog's warm burrow to fetch the feather down from her bed. When she returned to the tunnel, she spread it around the poor bluebird. He soon revived, opened his eyes, and chirped a happy song.

"Thank you, pretty maiden," he said. "Please, can you help me to escape from here?"

Thumbelina dug through the ceiling of the tunnel until a hole opened up and sunlight poured through. The bluebird roused himself, healthy now, and bid Thumbelina farewell.

Thumbelina waved good-bye to the bird and thought, *If only I could fly away, too!*

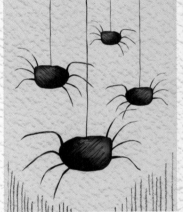

The very next day, the hedgehog had an important announcement for her. "The mole has chosen you for his bride," she said, clapping her small paws together with joy. "What good fortune for a poor little child such as you. Now, we must prepare your wedding dress." The hedgehog was so happy. "Oh, my darling Thumbelina, you will want for nothing when you are the wife of the mole."

The hedgehog hired four spiders to weave day and night. Thumbelina's dress would be a shimmering wonder. The mole would expect nothing but the best for his beautiful bride.

The mole now came by every evening. "When autumn comes, we will be married," he told Thumbelina. "We will

If only I could fly away, too!

spend the rest of our days underground, far from the terrible sun and sky."

As summer came to an end, the wedding day drew nearer and nearer. Thumbelina sadly resigned herself to a dark life underground. On the eve of her wedding day, she stood at the entrance to the hedgehog's burrow, drinking in the flaming colors of the evening sky and letting the last of the sun's rays embrace her one final time.

Tweet, tweet!

Thumbelina looked up, and there was the bluebird — her bluebird — sitting in a branch above her.

"Dear Thumbelina, come away with me," said the bird. "I will fly to a land in the south, where the sun shines more brightly and flowers bloom all year round."

Thumbelina's heart leaped with joy, and she readily agreed to his offer. She climbed upon the bird's back.

Then, with her tiny feet on his wings, the bluebird took off, soaring high above the burrow and away into the forest, far from the world Thumbelina had always known.

The pair flew for a long time, over snowy mountains, glassy lakes, and green fields that stretched as far as the eye could see. At length the air became warmer. They had reached the southern countries, where orchards and exotic gardens crowded among the small white houses along rivers that looked to Thumbelina like bright ribbons carelessly dropped onto the earth.

Eventually the bluebird set Thumbelina down beside a dazzling lake. In the distance there stood a palace of white marble. Vines clung to its sparkling walls, and at the top of the tallest tower was the bluebird's nest.

"There is my house," said the bluebird, indicating the tower. "But you would not be comfortable up there, so you must choose a flower down below. There you shall live and I will ensure that you have everything your heart could desire."

Thumbelina clapped her tiny hands in excitement. At last she was to have her very own home. She chose a large pink flower. It had delicate leaves and pretty petals, and it smelled of sunshine.

Just then, she heard the sweetest music coming from the neighboring flower. She crept closer and discovered a tiny little prince inside. He was singing a happy song.

"How beautiful he is," she said to the bluebird.

The little prince was delighted to meet Thumbelina. "You are the prettiest girl I have ever seen," he said. The two talked long into the night. Then he took the gold crown from his head and placed it on hers. He asked her to be his wife, princess of all the flowers.

The bluebird could see that Thumbelina had fallen in love, and his own heart broke, for he, too, loved Thumbelina. She had shown him such kindness when he was in the mole's tunnel. The noble bird bid the happy pair farewell and returned to his own home high up in the tower, where he could gaze down upon Thumbelina from a distance. He returned north every summer, and there he found a mate of his own. The two returned to the tall tower in winter and sang all day long.

THE END

Thumbelina's story is such a sweet tale. When I feel pushed around by the

world, I remember Thumbelina and take heart. No matter my size,

no matter my past, I have the power to choose my own future.

She teaches us to take life one small step at a time.

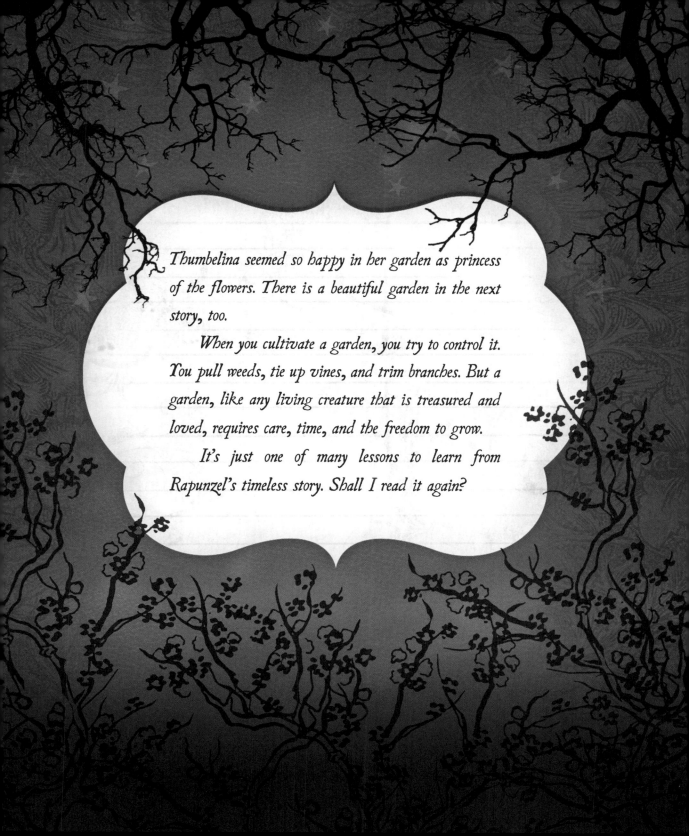

Thumbelina seemed so happy in her garden as princess of the flowers. There is a beautiful garden in the next story, too.

When you cultivate a garden, you try to control it. You pull weeds, tie up vines, and trim branches. But a garden, like any living creature that is treasured and loved, requires care, time, and the freedom to grow.

It's just one of many lessons to learn from Rapunzel's timeless story. Shall I read it again?

Rapunzel

There once was a man and a woman who lived in a pretty little house beside a towering castle. The house overlooked the castle's garden, the most spectacular garden you could imagine, filled with flowers and fruits of all varieties and colors. The land belonged to a very wealthy duchess, who was always planting new, exotic specimens; whenever she heard of some radiant blossom or succulent berry, she had to obtain one for her own unparalleled collection.

The man and woman would spend hours at the window, gazing in admiration at the duchess's garden, for no one could ever tire of such a dazzling array. Clouds of butterflies drifted about, drawn to the flowers' sweet perfumes, and full-throated birds sang in the thorny trees.

One night, the woman, who was heavily pregnant, looked out the window and saw that the garden was filled with rapunzel plant. She was filled with craving for this delectable treat and begged her husband to go into the garden to get some for her.

The man shook his head. The powerful duchess was protective of her garden. No one dared enter it, for severe punishment would surely follow.

His wife pressed him. "My dear, go. I want some of that rapunzel plant so very much."

When the man could no longer bear seeing tears in his wife's eyes, he finally agreed to go.

He crept over the wall and into the garden.

A voice cried out, "Who dares to trespass on my land?"

The man's knees quaked with fear as the duchess appeared before him. "Please, Your Grace," he said, "my pregnant wife desperately craves some of this plant, and you have so much of it growing here."

Although the duchess was a cruel woman, she was also a fickle one. The man had caught her in a good mood, and she considered his plea. "All right," she said at last. "You may take some of this plant, but in exchange you must give the baby to me."

In terror, the man agreed to the duchess's terms and returned with the plant for his wife. He did not tell her of the terrible bargain he had struck.

The wife gave birth to a lovely baby girl. She named her Rapunzel. The girl was a happy and caring child. The man 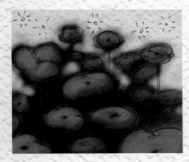 and woman loved her very much. She grew more beautiful every day, with magnificent, long hair. She liked to dance in the poppy fields near to the little cottage.

One day, in Rapunzel's ninth year, she stood at the window overlooking the duchess's garden with her mother and looked out at the splendor below. The woman embraced the girl and placed a tender kiss upon her cheek. They did not realize that they had been seen by the duchess, who was inspecting her plants in the garden. When she saw their quiet moment of affection, the duchess grew jealous of their love.

The duchess went over to the little house and insisted on taking the girl. The woman protested, but the man conceded that they were bound to the terms of their arrangement.

The duchess shut Rapunzel in a tower hidden deep in the wood, to ensure that her parents would not find her. The tower had neither stairs nor a door and only one window, high up among the clouds. Rapunzel cried for her father and mother. She wrote them letters, which she gave to the friendly birds who gathered at her window to deliver.

Five years passed, and Rapunzel's love for her parents stayed strong, but her memories of them slowly faded. She came to know the duchess well, for her captor was also her only visitor. When the duchess came to the tower, she would call:

"Rapunzel, Rapunzel,
Let down your hair to me."

When Rapunzel heard her voice, she would unfasten her braided tresses, wind them around one of the hooks of the window, and then drop her hair down to the ground far below. The duchess would then climb up it. She was determined to have Rapunzel's love — the love Rapunzel had shared with her mother — so she brought beautiful things to occupy the young girl and earn her favor. There were fine ribbons and darling buttons for dressmaking, sweet cherries and chocolates for baking, and a terrific assortment of toys. But best of all, there were books. Rapunzel loved to read, and she treasured each volume  in her growing library. She would read about far-off adventures, then spend hours at the window staring out toward the horizon, dreaming about the endless world beyond.

Two more years passed in this way.

Then, one afternoon, a prince rode through the forest and passed below the tower where Rapunzel sat sewing. He heard a song so charming that he stopped to listen. The prince wanted to meet the girl who sang so beautifully, but he could find no door to the tower. He returned home, only to come back the next afternoon, and the next, and the next, to hear Rapunzel sing.

Then one day he came earlier, in the morning, and he saw the duchess standing at the base of the tower. He heard her cry:

"Rapunzel, Rapunzel,
  Let down your hair to me."

Then Rapunzel let down the braids of her hair, and the duchess climbed up to her.

That is the way to reach the girl. I must try it myself, the prince thought. The next day, when it began to grow dark, he went to the tower and cried:

"Rapunzel, Rapunzel,
  Let down your hair to me."

He could find no door to the tower.

Immediately the hair fell down, and the king's son climbed up the tower wall.

Rapunzel was terribly frightened by the man who appeared in the window. But the king's son spoke to her gently. He praised her singing and said that his heart had been stirred by it; it let him have no rest. He had to meet the girl who sang so sweetly.

Rapunzel was calmed then, and she lost her fear.

The prince stayed late into the evening with Rapunzel, and they talked all night. Then Rapunzel became frightened again, because the dawn grew near and the duchess would arrive shortly. She hurried the prince away, but so charmed was he by the pretty girl with the long, long hair that he made her promise to let him visit the following day.

The prince came the next evening, and the next, and many days afterward.

Rapunzel and the king's son became friends, and slowly they began to fall in love. One day, the prince asked her to marry him and live with him in his father's castle.

Rapunzel's heart sang with joy, and she laid her hand in his. "I would willingly go with you, but I do not know how to get down," she said. "Bring ribbons with you every time you come, and I will weave a ladder with it."

The duchess knew nothing of the prince's visits. Then one day she came later, in the afternoon, to visit Rapunzel. She called up to her:

"Rapunzel, Rapunzel,
Let down your hair to me."

Rapunzel was so shocked to see the duchess — and not her beloved — climbing in through the tower window that she gasped, "Oh, I was not expecting you!"

The duchess flew into a rage and grabbed Rapunzel by the hair. "You wicked child! Whom have you been expecting, then? I kept you from all the world, and yet still you have become deceitful."

Rapunzel's hair fell to the ground.

She clutched Rapunzel's beautiful tresses, wrapped them twice around her left hand and seized a pair of scissors with her right.

Snip. Snap. Snip.

Rapunzel's hair fell to the ground.

The duchess dragged Rapunzel down from the tower through a secret passageway and led her deep into the forest. She left her there, mercilessly, for in time the girl was sure to be ravaged by wild beasts.

Rapunzel cried bitter tears over her own terrible fate, and she feared for her prince's safety.

The duchess returned to the tower and fastened the braids of hair she had cut off to the hook of the window. That same evening, the king's son came and cried:

"Rapunzel, Rapunzel,
  Let down your hair to me."

The duchess let the hair down.

The king's son ascended, but instead of finding his dearest

Rapunzel, he found the duchess, who looked upon him with hatred and venom.

"Aha," she cried mockingly. "So you would fetch your dearest! You would steal her away from me? But the beautiful bird no longer sits singing in the nest; the cat has got it, and it will scratch out your eyes as well. Rapunzel is gone; you will never see her again."

The duchess pushed him backward, and he fell down from the tower.

The prince escaped with his life, but the thorns into which he fell pierced his eyes. He was beside himself with pain and despair. He wandered, quite blind, about the forest for three days, ate nothing but roots and berries, and did naught but lament and weep over the loss of dear Rapunzel. The birds of the forest sang to comfort him, but still he cried.

On the night of the third day, the prince heard an owl hoot in a nearby tree. Alone and sad, with nothing else to do, he followed the sound.

Rapunzel was sitting on a log in that very clearing. As soon as she saw her prince, she leaped up and ran to him. She fell on his neck and wept. Two of her tears dropped down into his eyes, which grew clear again. He could see with them as before.

The prince led her through the wood to his kingdom. All rejoiced at their return, not least Rapunzel's long-lost parents.

Rapunzel and the prince were soon married, and they lived together always, happy and contented.

THE END

Rapunzel's joyful reunion with the prince is the perfect way to end this story — especially after such horrors.

My eyelids are feeling heavier by the minute, and a soft bed is waiting downstairs. It's time to turn in and say good-bye to this lovely evening.

Good night, Rapunzel, Alice, and Thumbelina! Good night, Little Red, Snow White, and the dear little mermaid! Good night to all!

The fairy tales are done, but the dreams are only beginning.